Pick-A-Path #4

The Amazing Bubble Gum Caper

by JANE O'CONNOR and JOYCE MILTON

illustrated by JERRY ZIMMERMAN

SCHOLASTIC INC.
New York Toronto London Auckland Sydney

ISBN 0-590-32893-X

12 11 10 9 8 7 6 5 4 3 2   2 3 4 5/9

Printed in the U.S.A.   40

READ THIS FIRST

Are you ready for some really fantastic adventures?

Start reading on page 1 and keep going until you have to make a choice. Then decide what you want to do and turn to that page.

Keep going until you reach THE END. Then, you can go back and start again. Every path leads to a new story!

It is all up to you!

Talk about boring summers! Your best friend has been shipped off to Camp Runamuck for eight weeks, and your mother has just told you that you will be baby-sitting for your pesky brother, Wilfred, every afternoon.

The most excitement you can expect all vacation will be adding to your collection of Gadzooks Bubble Gum baseball cards. You already have 6,573 cards, the biggest collection in all Goobersville.

Turn to **page 2.**

You take Wilfred down to your favorite newsstand and buy a pack of bubble gum for yourself and one for Wilfred, too. As usual, Wilfred opens his pack right away, and as usual, he won't show you what cards he got. You stop for a while and talk to Iggy, the news dealer. Iggy loves to talk. He can go on for hours about baseball. But today his mind is on other things.

"Check this out," Iggy says. He hands you a copy of the *Goobersville Gazette*.

"Wow!" you say, reading the headline.

STRANGE, PINK UFOs HEADING FOR EARTH SCIENTISTS BAFFLED

WASHINGTON—Scientists at the Mallomar Observatory have spotted a cluster of large clear pink spheres hovering over the capital city. Reports from New York, Chicago, and other major cities cite similar objects seen in the skies. . . .

Go on to the next page.

"UFOs? Come on. What is this, some kind of joke?" you ask.

Iggy shakes his head. "They're real, all right. It's just too bad these newspaper guys don't know the whole story."

You've heard this before. Iggy always claims to know the inside story on everything.

"Waaa . . . I'm gonna miss *Captain Comet* . . ." Wilfred is tugging at your arm. If he misses his cartoon show, he'll be in a bad mood all afternoon. What should you do?

If you stay to hear Iggy's story, turn to **page 4.**

If you're not in the mood for tall tales and think you'd better get Wilfred home, turn to **page 5.**

4   You figure *Captain Comet* can wait a few minutes.

"So what's going on, Iggy?" you ask.

"First, you must take an oath of secrecy," Iggy says.

"You can trust me never to reveal a word of what you say," you promise, trying not to smile. This looks like it's going to be a good one.

Iggy leans over the counter and looks right at you. "Those pink things they're talking about in the papers aren't UFOs at all," he whispers. "They are remote-controlled satellites launched by none other than" — Iggy pauses dramatically — "Buckley Bigbucks!"

Turn to **page 8.**

You take Wilfred home.

While he watches *Captain Comet,* you go to your room and get out the shoeboxes with all your baseball cards. You're hoping the pack of gum you just bought has some good cards but — rats! — they all turn out to be doubles of ones you already have.

Disappointed, you pop a piece of Gadzooks gum into your mouth and concentrate on blowing a bubble.

Wow! This one is a beaut! The bubble just keeps growing bigger and bigger and bigger. It's filling the whole room!

Suddenly — *pop!* — the bubble is gone and there is . . .

Turn to **page 13.**

You meet Chrissy at her office.

"Don't give away that card," she tells you. "It's all a hoax. There are no pink bubbles, and Iggy is no secret agent."

"But the newspaper said — "

"That was a fake newspaper Iggy gave you," Chrissy explains. "He had it made up just to fool you. See for yourself."

Chrissy hands you the copy of the fake paper she has taken from Iggy's newsstand. "There are too many silly mistakes for it to be real. You can see that for yourself."

Go on to the next page.

Weather Forecast:
Soup Tomorrow

June 31, 1993

★★ GOOFY ★★
GAZELLE

STRANGE, PINK UFOs HEADING FOR EARTH SCIENTISTS BAFFLED

quire advance preparation great technical skill. Spanish as set forth in this book, see mand the proper ingredien willingness to season with au

The recipes, often introdi diverting travel or historic : concise. I would question hours Mrs. Casac allowed dough to rise (mine took but not the entire head

wines and spirits tailored and availability in Americ menu suggestions, a glossa listing of sources for ingredie

Compared with those diseomed Spanish recipes, the for tralia, as presented in "Coo Colleen McCullough and ": those" (Harper & Row, $ frankly less appetizing. But Cullough, the author of "T

Mayor's Wife Opens Garden Club Show

Stay-at-home. can re-cre taste of Spain. The combir garlic, olive oil, ground alm the sausage chorizo, often addition of peppers and t readily telegraphs the robus flavor. And many of the re extremely simple.

Among the recipes that cou enlivon the regular family n appetizers of shrimp-sized ! oil and garlic er sausages si baked with pimento and win derful pancake style tortilla potato and onion, a versati and parsley; green sauce for and lamb cubes in garlic and

goofy (maple, crayfish, veal game passion fruit)

minute attention after a seri plicated preliminary steps a serve more than four. A reci ner rolls yields but five of th of wine or other cooking liqu be reduced to mere tablespor greens are warmed but not t

Plans Made for New Bridge

kitchens today, then it can compared to American cook 50 years ago.

Among its contents are : meat, beef stroganoff, Wald tomato juice, canned fruit (v fresh), sugared salad dress puddings galore. But this m ply be a reflection of the aut tastes.

This is a book recommende

Did you find 5 mistakes?
Then turn to **page 30.**

Buckley Bigbucks! He's supposed to be the richest man on Earth. Nobody knows what he looks like or even where he lives. In fact, no one has seen him in years.

"How do you know so much, Iggy?" you ask.

"I am not who you think I am," Iggy tells you. "I am an undercover agent." He flashes open his jacket to reveal a silver badge. It looks a lot like one Wilfred bought at the toy store.

Go on to the next page.

"I've been on Buckley's trail for a long time now," Iggy goes on. "Mr. Bigbucks is ready to blackmail the whole world to get what he wants."

"So what does he want?"

"I'm afraid I can't tell you that now," Iggy says, looking around nervously. "But I do need your help. Go to the video arcade tonight at six o'clock. You will get further instructions there."

Turn to **page 19.**

You arrive at the ball park just in time for the first inning. You look around at the crowd. Still no sign of Iggy.

"Pretty disappointing game," the bald man next to you says a while later.

"No joke," you agree. The Gnus are already losing to the Sweat Sox by seven runs.

Go on to the next page.

"Peanuts! Popcorn!" a voice shouts from behind you. You load up on several bags of peanuts and an orange fizz.

Hey, wait a second! The peanut vendor looks strangely familiar. As she's getting your change, you take a sip of soda and try to think. Finally you figure it out. She's the same woman you saw back at the arcade! But what's she doing here?

All at once everything starts to get *very blurry* . . . The last thing you see is the bald man next to you, grinning triumphantly. He must have slipped something into your orange drink!

Is this the last inning for you?

NO! Turn to **page 14.**

Iggy!

"How did you get here?" you shout. "Why are you dressed like that?" Iggy is wearing a glittery silver jumpsuit and a cape. The antennae on his head bob up and down when he moves.

"Do not be alarmed. Um . . . um . . ." He whips out a small booklet and flips through the pages.

"Oh, yes." Iggy reads from his booklet. "Do not be alarmed. I come on a mission of peace. I am an official Intergalactic Guardian of the Universe.

"I have been sent here to keep the Bubbleheads of the planet Gummo from destroying Earth," Iggy goes on. "If those pink bubbles pop, they will gum up your whole planet. You must help me while there is still time."

Is this for real? Probably not. But you decide to play along just to see what Iggy will say next. "How can I help?" you ask.

*Turn to **page 16** to find out.*

14   You wake up. Your head is pounding. It feels as if you just got hit by a hard line drive. "What happened?" you moan.

"We've been kidnapped," a voice says in the dark.

Your eyes begin to focus. It's that same woman again! The one who sold you the peanuts!

"I tried to warn you," she whispers. "But he got me, too."

"Who are you, anyway?" you ask.

"Chrissy Cross, cub reporter for the *Goobersville Gazette*. That news dealer you're so friendly with knows something about the UFOs, and I want to get the story before anyone else."

"Forget the UFOs," you say. "Where are we?"

Good question. To find out, go to the next page.

The door creaks open. Light floods in, framing the figure of a big, bald man.

"Good evening," he says. "I am your host — Buckley Bigbucks. Sorry I had to bring you here," Buckley says with a nasty laugh. "But with you in my power, Iggy won't dare spoil my little plan."

"What plan?" you and Chrissy squeak out together.

"You may not know it," Buckley says, "but I own the world's largest collection of baseball cards. The only player I'm missing is Homer Uhn."

"I know him," you say. "He only threw one pitch in the major leagues."

"Exactly," nods Buckley. "And there's only one Homer Uhn card in existence. Whoever has that card better fork it over in 48 hours, or I will explode my satellites. They're made from all the bubble gum I've bought over the years, and if they pop . . . well, need I say more?"

Looks like you and Chrissy are in a sticky situation. *Turn to* **page 22.**

16   "How can you help?" Iggy repeats your question. "Come with me to Gummo and talk to the Bubbleheads. My rocket ship is in the vacant lot behind your house."

No way, you think. If this is a joke, it's gone far enough.

But what if Iggy's not kidding? After all, there *was* a newspaper story about the pink bubbles. So wouldn't it be your duty as a good citizen to help in any way you could? What should you do?

If you're staying right where you are,
turn to **page 20.**

If you decide to go with Iggy,
keep reading on the next page.

You follow Iggy outside to the vacant lot. Hidden in some bushes is a small, rusty-looking spaceship. Iggy helps you inside.

Whoosh! The doors close behind you, and seconds later you blast off.

Soon you are hurtling through space. Planets and shooting stars whiz past the windshield. Wow, you think! This is better than *Star Wars!*

Then you see that Iggy looks worried. He keeps checking his pile of maps.

"Is something wrong?" you ask.

"I'm not sure which way to go," he says. "I think we may be lost in space."

"Oh, swell!" You should have known something like this would happen with a space cadet like Iggy.

"Don't worry," Iggy says. "I've been lost before. I remember the time I —"

"No stories now, Iggy!" you shout as a meteor nearly hits your spaceship. "We have to decide which way to go."

Turn to **page 18.**

Your spaceship is where the arrow is.
Draw a path through the maze to see
where you will end up.

Did you land on X?
Then turn to **page 56.**

Did you land on Y?
Then turn to **page 44.**

Did you land on Z?
Then turn to **page 26.**

You get to the arcade at six o'clock sharp. Iggy is nowhere in sight.

There's a woman in a trench coat playing Space Attackers. She seems to be watching you out of the corner of her eye. Minutes pass, but Iggy still hasn't shown up. You decide to play one game and head home. What a fool you were for ever listening to Iggy.

You drop a quarter into the Pac-Rat machine and wait for the game to start. But instead, the screen starts flashing:

GO SEE THE GNUS   GO SEE THE GNUS

Is the machine broken, or is this some kind of message from Iggy? The Goobersville Gnus are playing baseball tonight. On the other hand, there are also gnus at the zoo.

You've never helped out a secret agent before. What should you do?

If you go to the baseball park, turn to **page 10.**
If you go to the zoo, turn to **page 24.**

20   "Sorry, Iggy. Find somebody else to go to Gummo. I'm afraid I'm not cut out for the job."

"I've got to take *someone!*" Iggy sinks down on your bed and desperately leafs through his manual. "AHA! I found it!" He looks at you. "I hate to do this, but I guess I have no choice."

The stars on his antennae begin to glow, and suddenly you feel ice-cold. You cannot move a muscle. The next thing you know you are in the rocket ship, flying through outer space.

"How could you do this?" you shout.

"I didn't know what else to do." Iggy looks truly upset. "I'm sorry."

You feel movement returning to your arms and legs. "Well, being sorry is not enough!" You grab for the control stick.

If you push the control stick forward,
turn to **page 56.**

If you push the control stick backward,
turn to **page 44.**

You go straight back to the zoo.

Iggy pops out from behind a fountain. "Have you got the card?" he asks.

"Right here," you say, handing over your valuable Homer Uhn.

"The whole world will be grateful," Iggy says. "There are already 100 agents surrounding Buckley's hideout. When I deliver the card, they'll move in and arrest him." Iggy looks itchy to leave. "Well, I guess this is good-bye," he says.

"But can't I come with you?" you ask. "This secret agent stuff was just starting to be fun."

Iggy shakes his head. "No, it's too dangerous. I'm not even sure *I'll* make it out alive. But be sure to look at tomorrow's paper. You'll be the page one story."

"Good luck, Iggy. Be careful!"

As your words echo through the empty zoo, you wonder: Is this the last time you'll ever see Iggy?

To find out, turn to **page 54.**

Buckley leads you and Chrissy into the control room of his secret hideout. The walls are lined with television screens tuned to news reports from all over the world — New York, London, Tokyo, even Moscow. The whole world is wondering who has the Homer Uhn card.

"Only 47 hours and 23 minutes to go," Buckley says with a cackle. "And then . . . *pop!*" He points to a panel in front of him with one red and one blue button.

"Oh, dear," says Chrissy, "that card will never be found. We're doomed. Doomed!"

Is Chrissy right? Will the card ever be found? If you don't think it will,
turn to **page 50.**

If you think the card will turn up, turn to **page 28.**

Silly you! You didn't figure out that Bubbleheads get numbers backwards, too. Try turning the number 23 around, and you will be back on the right track.

24 You go to the zoo and head for the gnus. It is getting darker.

You think you hear footsteps behind you. Is it Iggy? When you turn around, you see a woman in a trench coat duck inside the monkey house. The same woman from the arcade! You decide to follow this mysterious lady.

Turn to **page 40.**

Could this be a secret message from Chrissy Cross? You try reading aloud the letters and the names of the pictures to see if they make any sense.

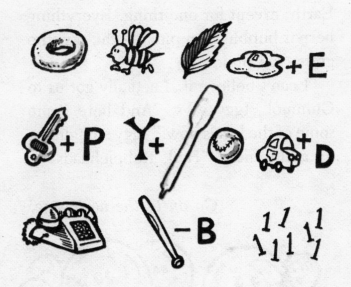

*Did you figure it out?
Then turn to **page 42.***

*If it's all still a bunch of doodles to you,
turn to **page 21.***

Your spaceship zooms into hyper-space. A few minutes later — or is it light-years? — the ship touches down.

You and Iggy get out and walk around. The planet you are on looks a lot like Earth, except for one thing. Everything here is bubble gum pink — the sky, the grass, the buildings.

"I can't believe it. I actually got us to Gummo!" Iggy says. "And here come some of the locals now." Iggy straightens up and salutes. "Hail, Bubbleheads!"

Go on to the next page.

Never in your life have you seen such a weird bunch. The Bubbleheads are very short, and you can see right through their huge, pink heads.

Iggy clears his throat. "I . . . I . . . I have brought a friendly Earthling with me," he stammers. "We are here to make peace between your two planets."

All the Bubbleheads laugh and giggle.

"I am Regor," says the first Bubblehead. "And this is Yram and Nevets."

What strange names! Then it hits you. If you spelled those names backwards, the Bubbleheads would be called Roger and Mary and Steven.

The Bubbleheads laugh some more and you smile back at them. They certainly seem friendly enough. But the next thing you know, Yram and Nevets step forward and clamp pink handcuffs on you and Iggy.

Turn to **page 49.**

No such luck! Almost two days pass and no one comes forward with the card.

And where has Iggy been all this time? You thought he'd try to rescue you! Some secret agent he turned out to be!

Now there are only 15 minutes to go before Buckley pops his pink bubbles. A waiter arrives in the control room with steak dinners for everybody. "Eat up," says Buckley, "this could be your last meal."

You are so nervous that you tear your paper napkin into pieces. Then you notice the waiter looking at you and pointing to the shredded napkin. You look down and see that there are words written on the torn pieces.

Oh, no! Did you tear up a secret message? Very carefully, you try to rearrange the pieces of paper.

Go on to the next page.

Is that it?

Maybe. But then you move the words around some more. Now they say:

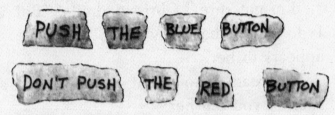

Oh, no! What should you do?

There are only 2 minutes left to decide.

*If you push the red button,
turn to* **page 46.**

*If you push the blue button,
turn to* **page 38.**

30   You look at the paper carefully.

"Yes," you say, "I see now that the date is wrong . . . so is the weather . . . and the title. There's a mustache on the lady and this picture is upside down! I guess this must be a fake. But why would Iggy play a trick like that on me?"

"I'm not sure," Chrissy admits. "But I do know that Iggy is not what he appears to be."

"I already know that he's a secret agent," you tell her.

"Oh, yeah? Take a look at this picture." Chrissy hands you a photograph of a bald man.

"Who's this?" you ask.

"It's Buckley Bigbucks. This is the only photo ever taken of him. Look familiar?"

"Not really," you confess.

Go on to the next page.

"Try drawing a mustache on the picture," Chrissy says. "Then add lots of curly hair, freckles, and glasses."

You do what Chrissy says.

Why, it's . . .

Turn to **page 39.**

Good for you! You knew when Regor said turn to page 23, he really meant go to page 32.

Now that you have Regor's backwards ways figured out, you think of a way to trick him. "I don't know what you Bubbleheads have against Earth," you say calmly. "And I don't want to know. Whatever you do, don't tell me."

Sure enough, just as you guessed, Regor does the opposite of what you ask. Soon he is telling you the whole story.

"We Bubbleheads do not like to be mean, but we are desperate," says Regor with a giggle. "Our whole planet depends on bubble gum. We must eat at least three packs a day to survive. But our supply is running out. Your planet has plenty of gum. Why, we hear that children on Earth chew gum just for fun and then stick it on the bottoms of chairs and desks when they get tired of it."

"That's true," you confess.

Go on to the next page.

Regor continues with his story. "We have used the entire supply from our last bubble gum mine to build the great bubbles that are circling over your cities. Unless you Earthlings agree to help us, we will set off the bubbles by remote control and . . . *pop!*"

You shudder at the idea. "Wait, I think I have an idea," you say, even though you don't. "But first you must take the handcuffs off Iggy and me."

The Bubbleheads whisper among themselves for a few minutes. Then Regor steps forward and sets you and Iggy free.

If you decide to make a break for it,
turn to **page 43.**

If you think you can help
the Bubbleheads and save Earth, too,
turn to **page 53.**

34   Way to go! You were smart enough to figure out that the sign was in mirror writing.

To avoid the dangerous Gummo swamp, you and Iggy turn left. You reach the spaceship, jump inside, and prepare to take off.

Soon you are drifting back through hyperspace toward Earth. Twinkling stars float past the windshield of the ship and make your eyes feel very heavy. Before you know it, you are drifting into a sound sleep.

Go on to the next page.

When you wake up, you are home in bed.

You sit up and shake the sleep from your eyes. You know that you were having a very weird dream about spaceships and pink bubbles. But you can't remember anything else.

You find Wilfred glued to the tube, watching cartoons.

"Come on, Wilfred," you say. "Mom doesn't want you watching TV all day."

You get dressed and drag Wilfred out the door.

Is this

THE END?

It could be,
or you can turn to **page 2.**

36 On the way to Elasticum, you stop for lunch. All the food in the restaurant is pink. The dishes look like they're solid gold, but that can't be. The Bubbleheads just throw them away once they've finished eating.

Regor makes a phone call. "It's good news," he says. "The Supreme Bubblehead will see you and Iggy."

Soon you are being led through the palace to your meeting. "I'm so scared," Iggy says. "I was better off working at the newsstand."

A booming voice over a loudspeaker interrupts Iggy. "The Supreme Bubblehead will see you now."

A pair of pink doors slides open. Propped up in a big bed surrounded by pink pillows is a very old and tiny Bubblehead.

"We come on a mission of peace," you say.

"*Achoo!*" replies the Supreme Bubblehead.

Go on to the next page.

While you are trying to figure out what to say next, the Supreme Bubblehead reaches for a shiny yellow tissue and blows his nose loudly. You notice that there are piles of used tissues lying around his bed, all of the same shiny color as the plates and cups they were throwing away at the restaurant.

"Excuse me, your, uh, Supremeness," you say. "But could you tell me what those tissues are made of?"

"Why, of course," he sniffs. "That's dlog. Our poor planet has too much of the stuff. Lately, every time we dig a bubble gum mine we run into dlog instead. We can't use it up fast enough."

Just what you expected. *Dlog* spelled backwards is . . .

Turn to **page 60.**

You hold your breath, lunge for the control panel, and push down the blue button.

"Hey! What's the big idea?" Buckley screams.

You wait for the popping sound, but there is none. Just sweet silence.

"You deactivated my bubbles!" Buckley cries. "That's not fair!"

Just then the waiter rips off his beard and false nose. It's Iggy! "You've schemed your last scheme," he tells Buckley. "My agents have this place surrounded."

Buckley is led off to jail as Chrissy scribbles away happily. "Wow," she says. "This is the biggest story of my career. No more covering pet shows for me!"

The next day you and Iggy are flown to Washington. You're going to meet the President and be the guests of honor at a ticker tape parade. You have become a national hero! And you thought this was going to be a boring summer!

THE END

"Iggy is Buckley Bigbucks!" you say. You can't believe it.

"Now we are going to find out what he's up to," Chrissy informs you. "I'm not going to let this story get away from me."

"But what should we do?"

"You go back to the zoo," Chrissy says. "I'll be right behind you. We'll play along with Mr. Bigbucks a while longer."

But when you reach the zoo, you are in for a big surprise.

Turn to **page 58.**

40   You race inside the monkey house. No one is there. The chimps are screeching wildly and pointing at the other door. Then you see a piece of paper on the ground.

It's a business card that says: CHRISSY CROSS. CUB REPORTER. *Goobersville Gazette.* On the other side of the card are some funny little drawings.

"What's that you have there?"

You spin around and see Iggy!

"There's a reporter spying on us," you whisper.

"Then we have to work fast," Iggy says. "You proved you can be trusted, so I'll tell you the whole story. Buckley Bigbucks is nuts about his baseball card collection. But he's never been able to get the Homer Uhn card. Now he's threatening to destroy the whole world unless someone gives it to him. There's only one in existence."

"But *I* have that card!" you exclaim.

Go on to the next page.

Iggy looks ready to faint. "I was pray-
ing you did. I know what a great collection you have." Then he gives you a
long, hard stare. "Are you willing to part
with it?"

"To save the world? Are you kidding?
Just tell me what to do."

"Get the Homer Uhn card and come
back here as fast as you can."

You run all the way home and search
through your baseball cards until you
find Homer Uhn. You are just putting
the precious card in your pocket for the
return trip to the zoo when you notice
that you still have the business card with
Chrissy Cross's name on it.

Something makes you turn it over and
take another look at those funny pictures.

Turn to **page 25.**

That's right. The message is:

> DO NOT BELIEVE IGGY.
> KEEP YOUR BASEBALL CARD.
> TELEPHONE AT ONCE.

Right away, you call Chrissy Cross at the *Gazette*.

"Meet me at my office immediately," she says.

"But what's going on? Can't you tell me?" you sputter.

"Don't ask questions. Just come." Chrissy hangs up on you.

You have never been so confused in your life. Whom should you trust?

If you decide to hear what Chrissy has to say, turn to **page 6.**

If you don't want to let Iggy down, go to **page 21.**

"Let's get going!" you hiss at Iggy.

Before the Bubbleheads can stop you, you and Iggy make a run for it. Behind you, there are sirens blaring and the sounds of running feet. You don't have much of a head start.

Soon you find yourself at a fork in the road. But which way do you run now? Left or right? You can't remember which way leads to your spaceship, and there is only one very confusing sign. It says:

If you decide to turn right,
go to **page 52.**

If you turn left,
go to **page 34.**

44   Your spaceship touches down. You climb out and find yourself in the middle of a cornfield. "It looks like we're back on Earth!" you cry out happily.

"Aren't you going to come back and help me find Gummo?" Iggy asks.

"Not on your life," you say. And off you run before Iggy can stop you. How long were you in space, you wonder? Your mother must be worried. Maybe you can find a phone and call home.

You get to a house and knock on the door. The lady of the house answers, only it is not a lady. It is a poodle!

"Oh, how cute," it says. "This little human must be lost."

"Mommy, Mommy," says a smaller poodle, "can I keep it for a pet?"

"What?" you shout. "This is all a mistake — I don't belong here!"

The big dog pats you on the head. "It almost sounds as if the human is trying to tell us something."

Go on to the next page.

Oh, no! You can understand them, but they can't understand you.

It looks as if you're stuck here on this crazy planet unless Iggy comes back to find you. You always *wanted* a pet, but you never dreamed you'd *become* one.

From now on, it looks like it's the dog's life for you!

THE END

Well, here goes, you think.

While Buckley is busy devouring his steak, you lunge for the control panel and push the red button.

A second later, you hear a loud *pop!* coming from somewhere outside.

"Hey, no fair!" Buckley whines. "I was supposed to do that —"

You never hear the end of Buckley's sentence. There are several more loud *pop*s, and then Buckley's secret hideout begins to shake and tremble.

It looks like this is it. Civilization is coming to a very sticky end indeed.

THE END

48   For some strange reason the newspapers make a hero of Wilfred! He is called "The Boy Who Talked Back to Buckley Bigbucks." No one seems to think your part in this caper was very important.

Oh, well, there's one good thing. Wilfred is now so busy traveling around the country appearing on TV shows, that you don't have to baby-sit anymore.

THE END

"Hey, wait just a minute!" you shout. "This is not my idea of a warm welcome."

"You are our prisoners now," Regor says. Then he sobs loudly as if this were the saddest thing in the world. The other Bubbleheads begin weeping, too.

What a silly bunch, you think. Bubbleheads laugh when they're angry and cry when they're happy. Is everything here the opposite of what it seems?

At last Regor wipes away his tears and makes this announcement: "To learn your fate," he says, "you must turn to page 23."

Your only choice is
to do what Regor says
. . . or is it?

50   You are wrong. The card is found. And guess who had it?

Wilfred!

He got it in that pack of bubble gum you bought him.

And there he is on the TV news. Wilfred does not look very happy about giving up the card. "No, no, no! It's mine!" he screams into the camera as your parents hand the card over to the police.

Five minutes before the 48-hour deadline is up, the card is delivered to Buckley's hideout. "At last!" he crows. "My collection is complete."

"But not for long," a voice says.

Go on to the next page.

It's Iggy! He and a team of agents storm into the hideout. Buckley Bigbucks is handcuffed. You and Chrissy are set free. Iggy even promises to see that Wilfred gets his card back.

Turn to **page 48.**

52   If you had held up a mirror to the sign, you would have found out that it was a warning to go left and keep away from the dangerous Gummo swamp.

Since you didn't figure out the backwards message, you and Iggy take the wrong turn. Soon both of you are wading knee-deep in pink-colored goo — and sinking fast.

"What do we do now?" you shout to Iggy

"*Glub, glub,*" is all you hear in answer.

Looks as if this crazy caper was one big mistake from the beginning right through to

THE END

"Take us to your leader," you demand.

"You mean the Supreme Bubble-head?" Regor asks. "But no one gets to see him."

Iggy is tugging at your arm, his antennae wobbling away. "Do you know what you're getting us into?" he asks.

"It's a little late to ask that now," you snap back.

"We will take you to the capital of Gummo," the Bubbleheads tell you. "Maybe the Supreme Bubblehead will see you, but then again maybe he won't."

Everybody gets into a long pink limousine. Regor puts it into reverse and off you go, backwards, all the way to the city of Elasticum.

Turn to **page 36.**

54   It *is* the last time you ever see Iggy.

The next morning you go to buy a copy of the *Goobersville Gazette*.

The headline is about the Goobersville Gnus' 0–10 defeat last night. But where is the story about Buckley and the pink bubbles? Where is your picture?

"So you gave away the card, did you?" You turn around. It's that lady in the trench coat, Chrissy Cross.

"Of course I did," you cry. "Buckley would have popped those pink bubbles."

"There never were any pink bubbles," Chrissy says coolly.

"But what about the newspaper?"

"That was a fake paper," Chrissy explains. "It was made up just to fool you. Here is the real paper." She hands you a copy of yesterday's *Gazette*. There is nothing about pink bubbles.

"He did it to get your Homer Uhn card," Chrissy says. "You still haven't figured it out, have you? Iggy isn't a secret agent at all, he's . . ."

Go on to the next page.

"Buckley Bigbucks!" It finally dawns on you.

Chrissy nods. "I tried to warn you. Buckley wanted that card and he got it — and I got a good story, too. Watch for it in tomorrow's paper."

Flash! Chrissy takes your picture.

Sure enough, when you check the paper the next day, there you are. Right on page one . . .

THE END

Oops! Bad move.

The spaceship is now completely off course. You are headed straight for a black hole. You will never reach Gummo, and you will never see Earth again, either. Your ship is trapped in a time warp.

"It's all your fault for getting me into this!" you scream at Iggy.

"Gee, I'm sorry," he says, thumbing through his instruction manual. "It doesn't say a thing here about avoiding black holes. If you think this is bad, you should have been with me the time I got lost in a snowstorm on the planet Frigidarus. It was nine million degrees below zero. No . . . that's not right. It was *ten* million degrees below zero . . ."

Iggy pauses to think it over. "Or was it only eight million? Anyway, here's what I did . . ."

Go on to the next page.

Great, you think, trying to tune out Iggy's voice. It's not bad enough that you're lost in space. You have to have Iggy for company. It looks like you'll be stuck listening to his boring stories forever . . . and ever . . . and ever . . . and ever. . . .

THE END

58   When you get back to the zoo, a big crowd has gathered. Giant spotlights beam yellow arcs across the sky. There are pink balloons everywhere.

Iggy steps forward to meet you. His wig and mustache and glasses are gone. Sure enough, he was really Buckley Bigbucks all along!

"I knew you'd come back," he shouts with delight. "For three years I have been searching for a child to star in my new movie *The Amazing Bubble Gum Caper*. I tried my pink bubble hoax on hundreds of children, and finally it worked on you."

Iggy/Buckley goes on. "Tomorrow you and your family will be flown out to Bigbucks Productions in Hollywood to sign a contract to star in my movie."

"Is this for real?" The question sounds dumb, but it's all you can think of to say.

"Perfect!" Buckley crows. "What innocence! That 'gee whiz' quality is just

perfect. Stay as you are, and you'll probably win an Oscar."

And you thought this was going to be
a boring summer!

THE END

GOLD!!!

When you tell the Supreme Bubble-head that you have a plan for getting Gummo loads of bubble gum, he is so happy he cries for two days. All the Bubbleheads give you and Iggy a big send-off.

Back on Earth, the two of you go straight to Washington to tell the President your plan. He thinks that trading bubble gum for gold is a wonderful idea. So do all the bubble gum companies.

The first interplanetary bubble gum shipment is sent that very week. A rocket is loaded with gum from all over the world — Gadzooks from America, Bubbalino from Italy, even Blutskaya gum from the Soviet Union.

Iggy is thrilled. He is going to get a medal from the Intergalactic Council. And you are welcomed back to Goobersville with a ticker tape parade and a key to the city. How does it feel to be a hero?

THE END